JUV/E Nixon, Joan Lowery.
FIC
    The Valentine
     mystery

Cop-1   R0055784134

DATE			

THE VALENTINE MYSTERY

Joan Lowery Nixon

Pictures by Jim Cummins

ALBERT WHITMAN & COMPANY, CHICAGO

Juv /E
Fic
Cop-1

Library of Congress Cataloging in Publication Data

Nixon, Joan Lowery.
The valentine mystery.

(First read-alone mysteries)
SUMMARY: Amateur detectives Susan and Mike track
down the mysterious sender of an unsigned valentine.
[1. St. Valentine's Day — Fiction. 2. Mystery and
detective stories] I. Cummins, James. II. Title.
PZ7.N65Val [E] 79-17055
ISBN 0-8075-8450-9

To my own Valentine, Hershell Nixon,
with my love

Susan saw the envelope on the hall table. "Who put this envelope here?" she asked.

"I didn't," Mrs. Connally said.

"Don't look at me," Mike said.

"My name's on it," said Susan. "I wonder what's inside?"

"Open it and find out," Mike told her. "Envelopes don't talk!"

Susan made a face at Mike. Then she opened the envelope.

"A mysterious valentine!" she said. "No one's signed it."

"It's a mystery why anyone would send *you* a valentine," Mike said. He grinned at his sister.

"Secret valentines are an old tradition
on Valentine's Day," Mrs. Connally said.
"It's fun to guess who sent them."

"The person who left this valentine must have been here just a few minutes ago," Susan said. "I heard someone knock while we were in the kitchen."

"Barney was in the living room," Mike said. "He must have opened the door."

Two-year-old Barney was sitting on the
floor, pulling at his shoes. "Take off
my tennis shoes."

"Barney, did someone come into the apartment?" Susan asked her little brother. "Did you see someone put this valentine on the table?"

"No," Barney said.

"It's no use asking Barney questions like that," Mike said. "He says no to everything these days."

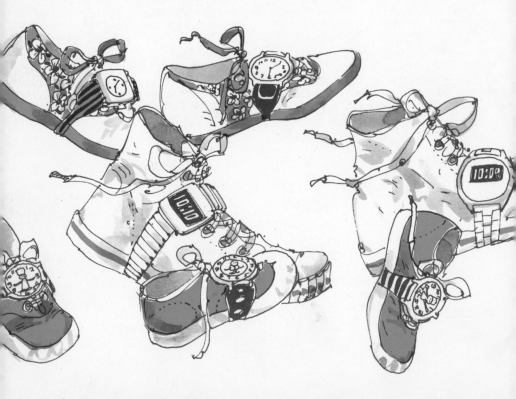

Susan tried again. "Who came into our apartment, Barney? What did he look like?"

Barney smiled. "He had watches on his tennis shoes."

"Watches on his tennis shoes!" Susan said.

"Barney's full of helpful information," Mike said.

"Come on, Mike," Susan said. "Let's ask
Mrs. Pickett if she knows anything about
this mystery. She lives right across
the hall. Maybe she saw someone come
into the apartment."

Just outside the door Mike and Susan met
Mr. Sasso. He did repair work for the
apartment building.

Mr. Sasso was stamping snow off his boots.

"Hello, my friends," he said. "It's cold outside."

"Hello, Mr. Sasso," Susan said. "Did you see anyone around who was wearing tennis shoes with watches on them?"

Mr. Sasso looked surprised. "No," he said. "I don't think I've ever seen anyone wearing watches on his tennis shoes. Not in my whole life."

"Well, let us know if you see someone with shoes like that," Mike said.

"I will," Mr. Sasso said. "I surely will."

Mike and Susan knocked on the door of
Mrs. Pickett's apartment. When Mrs.
Pickett answered, Susan said, "Do you
know who wears watches on his tennis
shoes?"

"Oh, good! A riddle!" Mrs. Pickett
said. She clapped her hands. "Let's
see . . . a spotted dinosaur who has
time on his hands?"

"No, Mrs. Pickett," said Susan, "It's —"

"Of course that's not the answer," said
Mrs. Pickett. "The tennis shoes wouldn't
be on his hands. They'd be on his feet.
I'll have to think about this. Come
inside and have some valentine cookies."

"Mrs. Pickett, did you see anyone in the hall this morning?" Susan asked.

"Yes, I did."

"Who?" Susan asked. "This is very important."

"Why, the two of you!" Mrs. Pickett said, laughing. "You were in the hall just a minute ago! You can't trick me. I'm much too clever."

"We have to go now, Mrs. Pickett," Mike said. "Thanks for the cookies."

"She wasn't much help," Susan said when
they were back in the hall.

Just then a boy named Pete came along.
He and his family were new in the
building. Pete was in Susan's class
at school.

"Hi," Susan said. She thought it would
be nice if Pete had given her the
valentine.

"Hi," said Pete. He looked at the floor
and hurried by Susan and Mike.

Susan looked at Pete's feet. He was
wearing boots with round buckles on them.
She wondered if he had on tennis shoes
under his boots.

"Wait!" she shouted after him.

Pete stopped. "What's up?"

Susan felt a little silly. "Under your
boots, are you wearing tennis shoes with
watches on them?" she asked.

"Your sister is crazy," Pete said to Mike.

"So what else is new?" Mike said.

After Pete had gone, Mike asked Susan, "What makes you think he'd give you a valentine?"

"Well, somebody did," Susan said. "We have to think of every possible suspect."

"Let's get our boots and coats and look around outside," Mike said.

At the front door they met the mailman. "Hi," Mike said. "Have you seen anyone around here with watches on his tennis shoes?"

The mailman stared at Mike. "I've never heard of tennis shoes with watches on them," he said. "And no one would wear tennis shoes in the snow."

He shook his head and began to put mail in the mailboxes.

"Let's walk down to the shoe store on the corner," Susan said to Mike. "Maybe the saleswoman can tell us something about tennis shoes with watches."

But the saleswoman was no help. "Some tennis shoes have stripes on them," she said. "And we have tennis shoes with flowers. But I've never seen watches on tennis shoes."

"Thanks, anyway," Susan said.

Susan and Mike headed home. As they came near the apartment building, Mrs. Pickett leaned out her front window.

"I've got the answer to your riddle," she said. "A spotted dinosaur wears watches on his tennis shoes because he's always running late!"

"No, Mrs. Pickett," Susan said.

"That's not the answer? Well, I'm not giving up. I'll figure this out yet." She closed her window.

Susan and Mike went into their
apartment. Mrs. Connally was sitting
with Barney, reading him a story.
"Take off your dirty boots before you
walk on the rug," she said.

Barney pointed to Susan's boots. "Dirty
tennis shoes," he said.

"These are boots, Barney," Susan said.

"Dirty tennis shoes," Barney said,
pointing to Mike's boots.

"Wait a minute!" said Susan. "Barney,
what does Mom have on her feet?"

Barney looked at his mother's fuzzy pink
slippers. "Tennis shoes."

"Right now Barney calls every kind of
shoe a tennis shoe," Mrs. Connally said.

"Tennis shoes . . . watches . . . if Barney
gets mixed up about tennis shoes, maybe
he gets mixed up about watches, too."
Susan said. "Maybe he just saw things
that *looked* like watches."

Susan thought hard. "Now I remember!"
she shouted. "I think we can solve
the mystery!"

Mike stared at his sister. Then he
grinned. "Right!" he said. "Come on!"

The two ran into the hall. Someone was
just hurrying out the front door.

"Stop!" Susan yelled.

The person turned around. It was Pete.
"What do you want?" he asked.

Just then Mrs. Pickett threw open her
door. "If the dinosaur had alarm clocks
on his tennis shoes, I'd say he was
alarmed!"

"That's not the answer, but thanks,
Mrs. Pickett," said Mike. "We've solved
the mystery now."

Susan turned to Pete. "Thank you for
the valentine."

Pete's eyes opened wide. "How did you
know it was from me?"

Susan looked at Pete's boots. Barney
must have thought the round, shiny
buckles were watches.

"Easy," she said. "We're detectives."

"Hey, Pete," Mike said. "Come on inside, I'll show you my model airplanes."

"Sure," Pete said. "Come on, Susan."

Susan smiled. She was glad Pete hadn't known what good detectives she and Mike were. It had been easy for them to solve this Valentine's Day mystery!